Christmas

By Robert B. Hoffman, Jr.

Illustrations by Josh Birdsall

Copyright ©1991
First printed in 1992
Second printing 1993
Third printing 1994
TXO 470 254

ISBN 0-9633156-0-9

Published By
Hoffman & Daughters
7761 Ingram Street
Anchorage, AK 99502
(907)243-0626

Printed in Alaska
By A.T. Publishing & Printing

Contents

1.) Little Tree

2.) The Most Beautiful Christmas Tree Ever

3.) The Painted Christmas Tree

4.) The Treasure Tree

5.) The Last Christmas Tree

6.) Big Tree

7.) Christmas Trees (PG- ∞)

PREFACE

Trees bring happiness

Managing a tree lot is not a piece of cake. Things that might go wrong for a person once in 10 years occur on a daily basis at the lot. It definitely is a place where "Murphy's Law" acts as a magnum force.

But somehow it's one of the most fun things I do each year. The rewards of selling trees come with each and every tree. A tree may cost $1 or $100, but it's still a Christmas tree and all the joy and happiness of the world come with it. When a person buys a Christmas tree you know it's an act of love and kindness. It's a thing for a special day that happens only once a year — a day of giving and receiving gifts and fellowship with others.

Selling a Christmas tree is almost like watching a person open up a gift that you have given them. Their eyes have a special twinkle when they see the tree's grace, and then they admire its beauty verbally. In their mind's eye you know they can see it in all its shining splendor on Christmas morning. If they have kids with them, their faces are glowing and their eyes are as wide and bright as they ever get. It's a magical moment with each tree.

After you sell the tree the usual season's greetings are exchanged, but the nice thing is that they always say "thank you." The greatest thing is that you know you are now a part of their happiness.

- Robert B. Hoffman Jr.

Christmas Memories

These pages are for you to record your own special Christmas memorie
—year by year, or a picture of your Christmas Tree that year.

LITTLE TREE

It was two weeks before Christmas and all through the tree lot the tree branches were stirring. All the Christmas trees were very excited because the next day was Saturday and many people would choose them for Christmas.

There were tall, elegant spruce trees, lovely scotch pines, and beautiful firs.

There wasn't a sense of competition among the trees because they had known from the time they had sprouted from seeds that they were destined to become Christmas trees. To a tree this is the highest honor of all.

As the trees rustled their branches in anticipation of the coming day, they all soon became aware of a tiny tree off to one side. It was not stirring a needle, let alone a branch. The stirring of branches ceased, and a big elegant spruce standing nearest the little tree asked him what the trouble was. The little tree replied, "Nobody will ever pick me for his Christmas tree because I'm too little."

The elegant spruce said, "Size has nothing to do with being a Christmas tree. You are one, and that's all there is to it. Because of your smallness, you will

Christmas Memories

have a very special place this Christmas. That's why you were harvested so small."

Soon it was morning, and the people who worked on the tree lot were there early. They carefully brushed each tree, cleaning away snow and frost.

Now in this country, it was customary that the King always had first choice of all the trees. The King would select twelve trees, one for each room in his castle.

All the trees were very excited, but the little tree wasn't excited at all because he was certain he wouldn't be picked.

Finally, the twelfth tree was chosen by the King; it was the big, elegant spruce nearest the little tree. As the man picked up the spruce, one of its limbs knocked the little tree over. The King saw it happen, and he picked up "little tree." "What a beautiful and graceful little tree!" exclaimed the King.

The King put his hand to his chin, and thought out loud, "I would love to have this tree, but where would I put it?"

Everything was very quiet for a moment, and then with a big smile on his face, the King said, "I know where I can put this beautiful little tree. Yes, yes, of course, I'll take this beautiful little tree."

The next morning, the big, elegant spruce tree

Christmas Memories

was standing at one end of the great dining hall in all its shining splendor. The spruce said, "You see, I told you you would have a special place." The little tree was beaming with pride because it was the centerpiece for the great hall table.

Christmas Memories

Christmas Memories

THE MOST BEAUTIFUL CHRISTMAS TREE EVER

One cold and snowy morning a long time ago, a young boy and his father were preparing to go and cut a Christmas tree. They saddled a horse and bundled up in warm clothes. The little boy was very excited because this was the first time he was allowed to go. He asked his father which way they were going, and the father replied, "About half way up the south slope of the mountain on the north side of the ranch."

"Are there many trees up there, Father?"

"Yes, Son," replied the father, "But there is one that grows all by itself in the middle of the meadow, and it's a beautiful tree. You can see it from here when it's not snowing."

"Is that the one we are going to cut?"

"I think so, unless we find a better one." With that the father lifted the boy onto the horse and climbed up behind him, and off they rode towards

Christmas Memories

the meadow.

When they arrived at the tree, the father climbed off the horse and lifted his son down. "Well, Douglas, here we are. There's the beautiful tree."

"Can I touch it, Father?"

The father looked into his child's eyes. They were the prettiest blue eyes in the world and filled with excitement.

"Of course you can, Doug. Give it a big hug."

The boy took his gloves off and put his arms around the tree.

"Oh, Father, it's so soft. It feels like fur, and it has a perfect shape."

"Yes, Son, it's the most beautiful Christmas tree I've ever seen."

The boy kept feeling the branches and exclaimed, "It's so soft, Father, and it smells so good."

The father untied the axe and said, "I'll help you cut it down, and we'll head back home."

"Wait a minute, Father! Did you say you can see this tree from our home when it's not snowing?"

"Yes, it's really not that far from the house. Look, there's your mother feeding the chickens. Yell to her;

Christmas Memories

she will hear you."

Doug yelled, "Hello, Mother!" and his mother replied, "Did you find a Christmas tree?"

"Yes, we did, Mother, but I don't want to cut it because it's too beautiful, and you can see it from the house."

"Then find another one that you can't see from here and return home before you catch a cold."

The father put his arms around his son and said, "I think you're right, Son. This mountain wouldn't be the same without this tree. Let's go into the woods and cut a different one."

"Oh, thanks, Father. I want this tree to live forever."

So they cut a different tree and headed home. On the way home, the boy asked, "Father, could we bring the little silver Christmas wind chime back up, and hang it on the tree in the meadow?"

"You bet, Son, we'll do it this afternoon."

That afternoon they took the wind chime back up the mountain and Douglas tied it to the tree. The wind was blowing gently, and the chime sounded its beautiful music. Douglas said, "Oh, Father, isn't it beautiful? This must be the most beautiful Christmas tree ever!"

Christmas Memories

The father hugged his son very tightly and said, "Yes, I think so too, and it will be forever."

On Christmas morning, Douglas woke up early and went to the door and opened it. The wind was blowing gently and it was just about daylight. He listened very intently, and then as though it were right next to him, he could hear the music from the chimes. He turned his head toward the tree, and in his mind he could imagine the glitter of the rising sun shining on the chimes and all the glistening snow flakes.

"Yes," he said to himself, "this is the most beautiful Christmas tree ever!"

He went to his parents' bedroom and woke them up. "Father, Mother, you must come and see the Christmas tree. It's so beautiful, and you can hear the chimes, too."

They went to the door and looked toward the meadow. By this time the sun was up, and they could see the reflection of the sun on the chimes, but they couldn't hear them. Douglas exclaimed, "Isn't the music beautiful, and look how beautiful the tree glistens in the sunlight!"

His parents, with tears in their eyes, listened as hard as they could, but they could not hear the chimes. His mother picked him up and hugged him, knowing that his hearing was much more acute than hers, said, "Yes, Son, it's so beautiful."

Christmas Memories

During Christmas dinner, Douglas said, "I would like to learn how to make wind chimes."

His father replied, "Why?"

Douglas said, "If I could make chimes, I would put a new one on my Christmas tree every year."

His father thought for a moment, and then said, "I think that's a wonderful idea. I'll see what I can do."

The next day father saddled his horse and rode into the village. He went to the blacksmith's shop and told Sam, the blacksmith, his story. Sam assured him that he could make some metal that Douglas could build chimes with.

Later, Sam went to the ranch house in his sleigh pulled by two horses with bells on them. Douglas went out to meet him and said, "I knew it was you, Sam. I could hear your horses' bells a mile away."

Father and Mother came out and welcomed Sam. Sam had a load of metal pipe in all sizes and lengths. Sam also brought a box of tools that he thought would help Douglas make his chimes. They took everything into the shop, and Sam explained to Douglas what each tool was for and how to use it.

Douglas couldn't wait to get started, so his father and Sam decided the three of them should build a set of chimes. They cut six pieces of pipe, all of different lengths, and then drilled holes through each

Christmas Memories

piece about four inches from the end. The holes were for the string that would suspend the pipe. The next step was to polish the pieces with sand paper. Each person had a different size of sand paper. Douglas had the finest sandpaper called emery cloth. He could tell when a pipe was finished because it felt as smooth as silk.

Soon, they suspended all the pieces of pipe with string from a round piece of wood about the size of a saucer, and hung a smaller piece of wood halfway down in the middle of the ring of pipes. On the center piece of wood, they hung a "tail" that would hang just below the chimes and catch the wind.

When they finished, Douglas held it up and blew on the tail. The music was beautiful, even his father and Sam were impressed.

Douglas exclaimed, "It's so beautiful, let's take it up to my tree."

They hung it on the tree, and the wind blew gently on it. Douglas said, "My tree is now the most beautiful Christmas tree ever."

When they returned to the house, mother was waiting with a big hug and kiss for Douglas and father.

The chimes were much larger than the little, silver ones, and everybody could hear them. It was beautiful. His mother told him how beautiful they looked in the sunlight. Douglas said, "Yes, Mother,

Christmas Memories

they look and sound just like an angel singing."

Time passed, and Douglas became a master chime maker, and each year, he would make a special chime to hang on his tree. People came from around the world to see and listen to the most beautiful Christmas tree ever. The chimes were polished so bright, that even at night, the reflection from the stars made the tree look like it was lit with a million candles, and the music was just as beautiful. Everybody who saw it said it was the most beautiful Christmas tree ever.

Many years later Douglas passed away, and they buried him at the base of his tree. His family removed all the chimes but one, the little, silver one. You see, Douglas never did see his tree. He only saw it in his "mind's eye" because he was blind. From that day on, every tree like "the most beautiful Christmas tree" is called a "Douglas fir."

Christmas Memories

Christmas Memories

THE PAINTED CHRISTMAS TREE

W hile travelling across a great desert, a wagon train came upon a very old Indian woman with long, white hair. She was by herself in a small teepee. When they came up to her, she waved her arms and asked them to stop. She started talking in her native language, and nobody could understand her.

The wagonmaster summoned one of his Indian scouts. The scout was from a different tribe and could only partially understand her, but he said she was starving and needed water. The wagonmaster told the scout to tell her she could share what food and water they had, and that she was welcome to come with them.

The scout gave her water and food, and helped her load her teepee and herself into a wagon.

During the next two weeks, they learned that her name was Sunwoman and that she was on a special journey. She learned from them that they had lost their way during a great storm and weren't certain

Christmas Memories

where they were. She also learned that they were very short on food and water, and would soon have to stop.

The children loved her because she would make little stone necklaces upon which she painted sunbursts in all colors with paints she kept in a leather bag. When the sun reflected from the painted stones, they shone like diamonds.

The next day, the wagonmaster told everybody they would have to stop and make camp until they could find water. That evening, all the people sat around the campfire and sang songs that were very strange to the Sunwoman. After singing for a while, one of the adults would read stories from a book. The stories thrilled the children, and this made the Sunwoman very happy. While the people were singing again, Sunwoman looked through the book. She saw pictures of a funny little man in a funny wagon with deer pulling it through the sky. She chuckled to herself as she continued through the book. The last page had a picture of a beautifully decorated tree with many gifts surrounding it.

The scout was always awake before sunrise, and he noticed that the very first shaft of sunlight that came over the mountain would strike Sunwoman's teepee first. The scout liked her because she was such a warm person, but he knew she wouldn't be with them much longer.

Christmas Memories

The next morning, the scout was watching when he first ray of sunlight came over the mountain. His eyes followed it, but the teepee was gone. He ran to he spot, but there was no sign of the teepee or of Sunwoman. He thought for a moment. He knew the sun would only shine here for a short time because t had risen over a low part of the mountain and would have to pass behind a higher part of the mountain before it could be seen again. He mounted his pony and rode southeast out of camp. He knew the direction was wrong for the wagon train, but he continued on. Soon, he urged his pony on faster, for he knew that very soon the first ray of sunlight would strike.

Suddenly, it was there, and to his astonishment, it was shining on a beautiful tree like the one he had seen in the book the night before. He knew there was magic there, and he rode on cautiously. When he arrived, he looked down into a beautiful sunlit valley with a river and green meadows. He climbed from his pony, got on his knees, and shouted with all his might, "E DEE HO!" In his language, this meant "where the sun comes down the mountain." He turned and looked at the beautiful tree again and mounted his pony and galloped back to camp.

He told the wagonmaster his story. The camp broke and everyone followed the scout. When they first saw the tree, the children all began shouting, "Look, there's our Christmas tree!" The closer they got, the more beautiful the tree became. When they

Christmas Memories

reached the tree, they couldn't believe what they saw. Everybody was very quiet. The tree was Sunwoman's teepee. She had painted it just like a Christmas tree, and when the sun hit it, it was as beautiful as any Christmas tree. It even had a beautiful angel on top of the center pole. The angel had long, white hair that glistened in the sunlight.

Then the people looked down into the beautiful sun-drenched valley with its river and beautiful green meadows. The people were overcome with joy and happiness. Tears filled their eyes, and they hugged and kissed each other.

When things settled down, the scout asked if he could give a prayer of thanks in his native tongue. The people fell silent, and the scout raised his arms toward the sun and again shouted with all his might, "E DEE HO!"

He held his arms to the sun until all the echoes from the mountains could no longer be heard. Then he turned towards the people and told them, "The 'Great Spirit' calls this place 'Sun Valley'."

As they started to leave, one of the children asked the scout, "But where is Sunwoman?"

The scout kneeled down, took the little girl's hand, and pointed towards the teepee, "She's in there, and her spirit will always be here in all of us." With that he held his hand over his heart.

Christmas Memories

"Can we look into the teepee?" asked the little girl.

"Yes," the scout answered, and opened the flap. There on the ground was a formation of painted stones shaped in the form of a beautiful sunburst.

Christmas Memories

Christmas Memories

THE TREASURE TREE

The man gave his wife a kiss and climbed upon his horse. He cinched the lead rope of the pack horse, put the other end around the saddle horn, and rode out of the yard.

It was the day before Christmas, and he had to find a Christmas tree. Normally this wouldn't have been a problem, but during the hot dry autumn, a forest fire had swept through the valley and destroyed everything in its path. The man's home and barn had been saved only because of a large plowed field that acted as a fire break. Everything else had burned. The crops and most of the cattle had perished. The other people had lost almost everything and had moved temporarily to a town near the valley, and, like the man and his family, were planning to move away.

As the man rode along, he was thinking that this was the second great tragedy of his life. The first was long ago when he was a boy. It was the day his father and uncle perished while working in their gold mine. There had been a terrible explosion, and the whole mine shaft collapsed. It was now their grave.

Christmas Memories

He remembered when his father, uncle, and himself would eat lunch outside of the mine and talk about where they were going fishing the coming weekend. He also remembered the day his father planted a little pine tree near the mine and told him that some day he should dig it up and replant it into the front yard of their home so that when he looked at it, he would remember his father and the mine.

The mine was at the end of a deep, narrow canyon, which had little or no plant life in it, thus ensuring that fire could not affect it. As the man neared the mine, he could see the tree, and he was thankful it was still there.

When he arrived, he tied up the horses, took a shovel, and began digging. Soon, the tree was free and he removed it from the hole. He wrapped some burlap around the roots and soil and then tied the tree onto the pack horse.

When he was about to pick up the shovel, he noticed something different in the hole. It looked like part of a saddle bag. When he tried to pick it up, it fell apart, and there before his eyes was a pile of gold nuggets. There was also an old, flat, tobacco can. He opened it and a yellow piece of paper fell out. He read it aloud. "Dear Son, your uncle and I thought you might need this some day. Love, Father."

A lump came to his throat, and tears filled his

Christmas Memories

eyes. He examined the hole again and found twelve saddle bags full of gold.

Because he was only one mile from home, he arrived quickly. He placed a wash tub in the living room and put the tree in it. It was probably the prettiest Christmas tree they had ever seen.

His wife and the children were going into town to buy things for Christmas dinner. He told her to invite all the neighbors who used to live in the valley for Christmas dinner because they had the only Christmas tree in the valley.

She replied, "How can we feed all those families when we can't even afford to put presents under the Christmas tree?" She saw a special sparkle in his eyes.

"It's Christmas," he said, "So tell them all to bring a special Christmas dish, and I'll take care of the rest."

After she left, he also left with two pack horses, each with a full set of paniers on them. When he arrived at the mine, he filled the paniers with as much gold as they could hold and then returned to the barn. There was still plenty of gold left at the mine.

He took several five pound coffee cans (which everybody saved in those days — for storage), and filled each one with gold. He then placed them

Christmas Memories

around the Christmas tree. They were very heavy, and he was almost worn out after his long day. Each coffee can had a Christmas greeting for the family, except for two. These two cans were taped together, one for the parson, and one to pay for rebuilding their church.

He covered the cans with a white sheet. When his wife came home, she asked what he had done. He showed her the note in the tobacco can and told his story. "If anybody asks," he said, "Tell them the sheet is supposed to look like snow around the base of the tree." She gave him a big hug and kiss.

On Christmas day, the neighbors arrived, and dinner was served. After dinner, the man asked everyone to come into the living room. He told them how much he loved the valley and the people who lived there.

Then he asked them if they would stay in the valley if they could afford to rebuild their homes, the school, and the church. They all agreed they would stay. He told them about his father asking him to replant the tree in the front yard. Then he removed the sheet and asked a young boy to pick up the coffee can with his family's name on it. The boy tried, but he couldn't lift it. The boy's father also tried to pick it up and said, "This is too heavy."

The man told him to open it. He did and with a shocked voice said, "I can't believe it."

Christmas Memories

The man told them the rest of the story and showed them the note from his father. As each family opened its can of gold, there were tears of happiness, and many hugs and kisses.

After the parson gave a prayer of thanksgiving, they all agreed to rebuild the church and their homes and return to the valley.

They all agreed to become Christmas tree farmers too!

Christmas Memories

Christmas Memories

THE LAST CHRISTMAS TREE

Christmas Day was only a couple of days away, and many people were coming to the Christmas tree lot to choose their tree. Most of the trees had been chosen earlier, and there were just a few left. One by one the trees were taken until there was only one left.

The tree had been picked up and brushed off many times, and some of its branches were broken. It was in very bad shape.

It was the day before Christmas, and the man who owned the tree lot put out his closed sign early. He took the last tree and stuck it in the snow near the sign and wrote "free" on its tag.

He knew it would be gone in the morning. The last tree always was gone on Christmas morning. But he never knew where it went.

It was soon dark, but the night sky was brightly lit with millions of stars. A big one in the east was shining more brightly than all the others.

All the houses in the village were brightly lit with Christmas lights, except for one. A very small house

Christmas Memories

at the end of the town had nothing but a single candle burning in the window. The people who lived there were very poor, but they were good people who worked very hard for what they had.

The father was a handyman in the village, and in his spare time he liked to write stories. Earlier that year he had even sent some stories to a publisher.

Except for what the villagers gave them, the children at this home never received much for Christmas. But they knew the true meaning of Christmas, and that was enough for them.

If trees had feeling, the last tree felt very bad. Nobody had chosen it, and nobody probably would.

Suddenly a bright shaft of light coming from the bright star in the eastern sky completely illuminated the tree, and then three angels appeared. One of them picked up the last tree and kissed it on the very tip. The tree was instantly transformed. Its branches were all intact and perfect, and every needle shone as brightly as any Christmas light ever had.

The angels looked toward the village and noticed the last, little house with just one candle in the window. They nodded to each other, picked up the tree, and went to the house.

They entered the house and looked around. One angel placed the tree in the corner of the room, and

Christmas Memories

all three angels decorated it with their magic touch, as only angels can do. The tree was absolutely beautiful when they finished. Then each angel searched a different part of the house looking for things like warm boots, coats, hats, toys, and food.

When they returned to the room they were all smiling for they had found one thing that was not needed, and that was "love" because there was evidence of this everywhere. This made their job very easy because with love anything can happen.

The angels knew what was missing, and with their magic touch they went to work.

Gifts were placed around the tree, food was stocked in the cupboard, and one angel even put a Christmas dinner in the oven.

The angels looked around and decided their job was finished and they left. As they were flying from the house, one of them swooped down to the mail box and touched it. Instantly a beautiful golden ribbon appeared around it.

When morning came the mother awoke first. She thought she smelled something cooking and went to check on it. When she walked into the room she saw the beautiful Christmas tree and all the gifts. Tears filled her eyes, and she bowed her head and said a prayer of thanks.

She thought her husband had done all this and

Christmas Memories

she returned to the bedroom and woke him with a lovely kiss. She said, "Let's wake the children. They will be so surprised. It's wonderful."

The children went into the room with the Christmas tree and with wide eyed curiosity walked towards it. The Christmas tree was so beautiful they hardly noticed the gifts. They had never had a Christmas like this before. They weren't sure that it. wasn't just a dream.

Then they saw their names on the gifts. They looked at their mother, and then turned and ran to their father to hug, kiss and thank him.

Father was as surprised as everyone else, but he went along with it, enjoying everything more than any Christmas in his life.

The gifts of coats, boots, hats, dresses, mittens, dolls and other toys were all opened. Mother and the girls asked "But Father, where are your gifts?"

Father wasn't concerned about a gift, because he had the greatest gift in the world — "love." With tears in his eyes, he gave all three of them big hugs and said, "You are my gifts because you are my family."

The father was trying to think of an explanation when one of the children exclaimed, "Father, look at the mail box! It has a beautiful, golden ribbon around it. I'll bet your gift is in it!" She ran to put on

Christmas Memories

her new hat, coat, and boots, and ran through the snow to the mail box. She opened it, and took out a golden envelope addressed to her father.

Everyone wondered what it was. Father opened the envelope and unfolded the letter. Inside was a check for a very large amount of money.

The letter read:

Dear Sir,

Thank you for asking us to publish your stories.

We hope you will accept this check as partial payment for your work.

Merry Christmas,

Three Angels Publishing Co.

P.S. We liked your story about "The Last Christmas Tree" the best.

Christmas Memories

Christmas Memories

BIG TREE

Once upon a time on a Christmas tree farm, a young lady working with the seedlings noticed that one tree was almost twice as big as all the other seedlings. The lady pointed the tree out to the other workers and they all agreed that this might be a very, very special tree. The lady said, " If we're lucky this might some day be "the one."

Trees growing on a tree farm must be replanted many times when they are young. This is to insure that each tree has enough space to grow without interference from other trees, so that their branches grow even all around. Each year "Big Tree", (the name given the large seedling) was replanted in a place where it had plenty of room to grow because it was so much bigger than the other young trees.

In the spring of each year Big Tree watched as the fields around him were planted with new young trees. This was Big Tree's favorite time of year because it was time to grow some more and he could feel the life flowing from the tip of his roots to the top tip of his trunk and back again. "Xylem up and phloem down," he would chuckle to him-

Christmas Memories

self. Every needle on every branch absorbed the light energy from the sun, and his roots absorbed the water from the warm rains that soaked into the earth. Yes, for the next few months Big Tree would grow and grow and grow.

After several years of growing and replanting, all the trees were moved to a very large field. Big Tree was planted in the center of the field with lots of space around it so it would get plenty of sunlight and grow straight and tall. This field would be the final place for this group of trees to grow until they would be harvested for Christmas.

Each year while the trees were growing, the farm workers would prune their branches and shape them so they would become more beautiful as they matured. Big Tree was given special attention, almost pampered, by the lady who discovered it. She would spend long hours pruning and shaping it until she was absolutely satisfied that the tree was as beautiful as it could be. Then she would say, "Some Christmas you are going to be "the one" Big Tree, I just know you will."

There were many different fields with trees of different ages and sizes, on the farm. Each year selected trees from each field were harvested and shipped to market in many cities and towns during the Christmas season. Some people want small three foot trees, some want medium four to five foot trees, and some want large six to eight foot trees. Most of the trees are harvested by the time

Christmas Memories

they are eight feet tall, but a few are left to grow taller for those few people who want a very large tree. So large or small, short or tall, everybody can have a beautifully shaped tree of their choice.

Many trees had been harvested from the field where Big Tree was growing, until at last, all the trees it had been planted with were gone and new trees had been planted in their places. Now, Big Tree was nearly forty feet tall and still growing.

The little trees in the fields wondered why Big Tree never went to market, and they would ask him all kinds of questions about it. Big Tree didn't know the answers, so he was embarrassed and sad when the little trees would make fun of him by saying that he was too big and too old to ever become a Christmas tree.

When the workers pruned the trees, it would now take them several days to do Big Tree. They now had to use ladders and ropes, and be very careful so they didn't break any of his limbs. When they were finished, they would stand back and admire how straight, tall and beautiful Big Tree was.

The lady worker who first discovered Big Tree was much older now and she had raised a family of her own. She told her son and daughter how she had found the tree when she was young and that she knew when she first saw it that it was a special tree. "Maybe if Big Tree keeps growing straight and tall for the next ten or twelve years we'll get lucky and it will be "the one", " she said.

Christmas Memories

As the years passed the younger trees still asked Big Tree questions about why he was never harvested, and taunted him with jokes. One little tree yelled, "What are you going to be Big Tree, a telephone pole?"

Another one said, "Yeah, more power too you Big Tree!"

All the trees laughed, even Big Tree had to chuckle sometimes, but he thought, a telephone pole —- power lines —- YUCK!

A few years later when the harvest season started in the fall, Big Tree was again watching the other trees being selected when a strange thing happened. A farm truck and a large black limousine came up the road to Big Tree and stopped. The lady who discovered Big Tree got out of the truck and escorted the people from the limousine around Big Tree. The people were walking all around Big Tree, looking, talking and taking pictures. Finally they were all laughing and shaking the lady's hand. She was half laughing and half crying and saying very loudly, "Thank you, thank you, it's so wonderful, I'm so happy — I knew someday Big Tree would be "THE ONE"!"

The people got in the limousine and left. The lady reached into the truck's window, pushed on the horn and yelled to all the workers to come over to Big Tree. When everybody was there she announced that Big Tree had been chosen "THE ONE"! Everybody began cheering, dancing up and down

Christmas Memories

and hugging each other! When things quieted down, the lady said, "Let's sing a song to Big Tree, let's sing "O, CHRISTMAS TREE — O, CHRISTMAS TREE"!" Big Tree and all the other trees on the farm could only wonder what all the excitement was about. There never before had been any singing and dancing for any other tree on the farm.

That night all the other trees were guessing what was going to happen to Big Tree. "Maybe there are some giant people who live in a very big house," said one tree. Some others thought he was going with the circus, and some thought they were going to put him on the moon so the whole world could see a Christmas tree. Big Tree shuddered at the thought of being on the moon —he liked good old Terra Firma just fine.

The next morning a parade of big trucks and other equipment, including a crane, arrived at the farm. A large backhoe began digging up the ground around Big Tree's roots, a cable was secured to his trunk, and soon he was lifted by the crane from the ground and laid onto the bed of a very long truck. His roots were covered with wet cloths and then the whole truck bed was covered with tarps. It was dark as the inside of a cow, and because he was laying down he felt like his sap was running in every direction at once. Big Tree was scared!

As the truck started moving he could hear all the other trees saying goodbye, "See ya Big Tree, bye

Christmas Memories

Big Tree, good luck, see ya on the moon Big Tree!"

"Oh no, not the moon! Any where but the moon," Big Tree said to himself, and with that thought he fell asleep.

The two drivers drove the truck for several days before they reached their destination. Big Tree couldn't stop thinking about the moon! When the truck finally rolled to a stop, the tarps were removed and Big Tree was immediately lifted by a crane and placed into a very large hole. Fresh soil was shoveled and tamped around his roots, and lots of fresh water was sprayed all over him.

It felt good to be standing up again. He looked all around and didn't recognize anything, but he was pretty sure he wasn't on the moon. That was a relief! There were lots of other trees but none like him. They were weird looking, shaped funny, and not green at all. None of them had needles, but some had a few bright red and yellow leaves left on them. They were all looking at Big Tree.

Finally Big Tree said, "Hi, I'm Big Tree, I'm a Christmas tree!"

A huge tree with great big limbs bellowed, "Howdy, I'm Acorn, I'm a mighty oak!"

Others said, "Welcome, I'm Shady, I'm an elm!"

" Good day, I'm Shagbark, I'm a hickory!"

"Yo, I'm Nut, I'm a beech!"

"Good Morning, I'm Syrup, I'm a maple!"

"Konnichiwa, I'm Blossom, I'm a cherry!"

Christmas Memories

"Greetings, I'm Candle, I'm a bayberry!"

The introductions went on and on until every tree in sight had said hello. All the trees were very pleasant and polite with sort of a reverence that made Big Tree feel especially important and very welcome.

A few days had passed and many people stopped by to admire Big Tree. Most of them were coming from and going to the many big buildings near by. One man in particular, (who was escorted by several men that never smiled), strode around him several times, admiring his beauty. The man congratulated some of the people for finding such a pretty tree, and remarked, "this "one's" great!"

About a week later trucks came and men in boxes were lifted up by a crane's arm to the top of Big Tree. The men, with several people on the ground helping them, began spiraling tree lights around Big Tree from top to bottom. Then came hundreds more large, small, shiny and bright decorations of all different kinds hanging from his boughs. Big Tree was so happy, at last he was a Christmas tree.

The next day still more people were busy building a platform near him, while others were setting up big cameras and lights. It started snowing and by evening there was a light snow fall on everything.

When it became dark a large crowd of people began gathering around Big Tree. People came from

Christmas Memories

the buildings and the streets. Everybody seemed filled with anticipation, they were laughing and shouting to each other, and some were singing Christmas carols while an orchestra was playing.

Soon the stage was set and some people walked on to the platform. One man asked the crowd of people to be quiet. "Quiet, quiet please everybody!" When everybody was quiet, the man said, "Welcome to our Christmas tree lighting ceremony, and Mr. PRESIDENT would you please light the tree!" The President pushed a button and Big Tree lit up just like a Christmas Tree, in fact, he was "THE ONE", the NATIONAL CHRISTMAS TREE! The only "ONE" that was chosen from all the other trees in the whole United States! WOW! WHAT AN HONOR!

Everybody was clapping their hands, oohing and aahing and yelling Merry Christmas to one another! The President asked the crowd to be quiet again, and the orchestra began playing "O,CHRISTMAS TREE — O,CHRISTMAS TREE" and all the people sang along with the beautiful music.

Big Tree was very proud and he thought to himself, "Gee, I wish all the people and the young trees on the farm could see me now!" Well, they could see Big Tree because all the people on the

Christmas Memories

farm were watching him on T.V., and they were all so happy and proud that the NATIONAL CHRISTMAS TREE was from their farm. In fact people all over the United States could see Big Tree on T.V. that night —- maybe you saw him too.

Some of the trees near the farm house could see the T.V. through a window and one yelled, "Look there's Big Tree —- he's a Christmas tree and he's beautiful!" "Is he on the moon?" "No, he's in the house in a box!" —- "How you do dat?" asked a young tree.

Anyway Big Tree is still there on the White House lawn, and if you are ever there and you see him, say, "Hello Big Tree, I read a story about you," and don't forget to tell him he's beautiful —- he loves it!

Christmas Memories

Christmas Memories

CHRISTMAS TREES
(PG - ∞)

Legend has it that Martin Luther is given credit for decorating an evergreen tree to celebrate Christmas with his family, way back, whenever, in Germany.

Since then Christmas trees have become a wonderful tradition around the world at this very special time of year.

Each year the Christmas tree brings nostalgic memories of Christmas past and sets the stage for Christmas present.

The "inner child" in each of us is conjured by the Christmas tree's exquisite magical charms, and we each respond in our own puerile ways.

The green colored pyramid shape of the Christmas tree is pleasant to look upon, and maybe suggests a sense of refuge, peace, and serenity for the human spirit.

Our olfactory nerves are stimulated by the aromatic fragrance that permeates our homes when a Christmas tree is placed within, and most of us adore that "piney" bouquet, it's fresh, clean, and perhaps a little wild.

Of course all Christmas trees are not "real", or

Christmas Memories

of the natural conifer variety.

Artificial or "plastic" trees, made from petroleum resins, are nearly as popular as real ones. Which one has a pedigree of greater entity?

Who ever thought that a diatom, an itsy-bitsy prehistoric life form that lived in an ancient sea would someday become part of a Christmas tree.

Wow! That's a dynamic pedigree!

In Appalachia sometimes small hawthorn trees are painted gold, silver, green or many other colors, and then gum drops of all colors are impaled on their thorns to create simulacrum Christmas trees.

Near the northpole, (Santa Land), there aren't trees of any kind so the antlers of caribou and moose are often stacked in the shape of a tree and decorated with skins, bones, ivory, fur, lights and other ornaments to become a Christmas tree.

Probably many things have been used to simulate Christmas trees, but whatever it might be, real or artificial, large or small, it's still a Christmas tree, bringing a maximum amount of happiness and joy to all.

How do you decorate a Christmas tree? Do you do it with TLC, precise placement, random tossing, absolute conviction, or artistic ability? Who cares? Every body is an expert with a natural affinity for decorating a tree, and if you don't believe that, just ask the person doing the decorating .

Once the tree is decorated and lighted with a

Christmas Memories

biblical star or angel on top, its magnificent splendor shines into the hearts of all who know the true meaning of Christmas.

I like to think that each and every lighted Christmas Tree in the world is like a birthday candle for a very, very special birthday —-
CHRISTMAS!

Christmas Memories

Christmas Memories

About the Author

This is the first written collection of stories by Bob Hoffman, but he has been a master of the lost art of oral story telling since he was a teenager. He grew up in an old sleepy Ohio River town a lot like Mark Twain's Hannibal. Although he was a natural athlete, as a a youth he was drawn to the area's woods, rivers, and lakes. He became an accomplished and locally well-known outdoorsman. He had a sensitivity to the mysteries and spirits in special natural places, animals, and even inanimate things. Bob also has a gift for expressing his vision of the natural world by telling stories that hold listeners spellbound. Talking trees and magical tepees become natural and believable. Publishing these stories is a natural step in his growth as a storyteller.

After college he taught biology in high school and colleges in Ohio. He left there in 1971 for Jackson, Wyoming, and moved to Anchorage in 1978 where he has been a carpenter. He and his wife, April, have two daughters, Kista and Kassi.

Richard P. Schneider

About the Artist

Joshua Birdsall has made his home in Anchorage, Alaska, since 1975. He graduated from Dimond High School in Anchorage and is presently in his first year as an art major at Oberlin College in Ohio. Joshua has been an active artist since childhood. He has shown his work at Artique, Ltd. in Anchorage, has won several awards in juried exhibitions, and his work was featured in National Scholastic Magazine in 1991.